THE PHOENIX
ON BARKLEY STREET

ZETTA ELLIOTT

THE PHOENIX ON BARKLEY STREET

PICTURES BY ENROC ILLUSTRATIONS

Rosetta
Press

BOOKS BY ZETTA ELLIOTT

A Wish After Midnight
Bird
Max Loves Muñecas!
Room in My Heart
Ship of Souls
The Boy in the Bubble
The Deep
The Girl Who Swallowed the Sun
The Magic Mirror

1.

Carlos is my best friend. We live on Barkley Street.

Barkley Street used to be an okay place to live. There was a park at the end of our block, and families lived in all the houses along our street. Each summer we held a block party with cool music, fun games, a talent show, and lots of great barbecue!

Then, as we got older, Barkley Street started to change. Some of the families moved away. The

empty houses were boarded up. The swings in our park were broken and never fixed. Graffiti sprawled across the walls like spiders. The grown-ups got so scared they decided to cancel our annual block party.

Barkley Street changed, but Carlos and I stayed the same. We passed the park every day on our way to school, but we never went there to play. Older boys hung out and played loud music on their stereo. Sometimes they tried to talk to us. Carlos and I pretended not to hear.

One day as we were walking home from school, Carlos told me a secret.

"I found a new place for us to hang out," he said.

Carlos had that look in his eye. I knew he was up to something.

Carlos led me to the end of our block. We

stopped in front of an abandoned building. All of the windows were boarded up. The front door had been sealed with bricks. The stoop was hidden by a tangle of trash and weeds.

I looked up at the ugly old building. "Man, we can't hang out here."

Carlos looked around to see if anyone was watching. "Follow me," he said.

We went around the corner. The crumbling building had a long backyard that was surrounded by a tall wooden fence. The fence was covered in ivy. There was a coil of razor wire running along the top.

Carlos looked around one more time, then pulled aside the curtain of ivy. There was a narrow crack in the wooden fence.

"Take a look and tell me what you think," he said.

I peered through the crack in the fence. At first all I saw was long grass that looked like it hadn't been cut in years. Then I saw a soggy mattress, several broken chairs, and a table turned over on its side. I saw overgrown rose bushes, an apple tree, and a pear tree. The ground beneath the trees was covered with rotten fruit that gave the yard a sickly-sweet smell.

I stepped away from the fence and looked at Carlos. "Man, are you crazy? It's like a jungle in there!"

Carlos just grinned at me. I could tell how excited he was.

"C'mon, Tariq," he said. "It may look like a jungle now, but imagine how it'll look once we clean it up."

"Clean it up!" I exclaimed. "It'd take weeks for us to clean up that mess."

Carlos kept on grinning. He knew that I was interested and that I would help him fix up the yard.

"Let's get here real early tomorrow morning," Carlos suggested. "That way we can get into the yard without anybody seeing us. This will be our secret hang-out spot. Deal?"

As I shook hands with Carlos, a tingly feeling of excitement ran up my spine. We looked at each other and smiled. "Deal!"

Early the next morning, Carlos and I met at the end of the block. Since it was a Saturday, most of our neighbors were still asleep. Barkley Street was quiet and still. Carlos was carrying a black duffel bag. I had my father's crowbar and my mother's garden rake.

"Alright," said Carlos. "Let's do this."

We went around the corner. Carlos kept watch

while I used the crowbar to loosen two of the planks in the old wooden fence. After pushing the bag and the rake inside, Carlos and I crawled through the opening we had made in the fence. We fixed the two planks from the inside so no one on the outside would know how we got in.

Once we were inside, the yard didn't look so bad—it looked worse!

Carlos unzipped his duffel bag. He took out two pairs of gardening gloves, a pair of shears, and some plastic garbage bags.

"Let's get to work," I said.

Carlos and I took turns cutting the long grass with the shears. We raked up the fruit that was rotting on the ground. We filled three garbage bags with trash people had thrown over the fence.

After a while Carlos and I sat down to take a break. The sun had risen over the treetops, and it was starting to get hot. In his duffel bag Carlos had brought a box of cookies and two bottles of juice. As we ate, a bird began to sing. Carlos and I sat still and listened.

I had never heard a song like that before. It was sad, but also beautiful. The bird sounded like it came from a faraway place, but the music was loud and clear.

Carlos looked at me. "What kind of bird is that?"

I shrugged and got up from the table. "It sounds like it's coming from over there."

I walked towards an old oak tree that stood in the far corner of the yard. I couldn't see a bird, but the singing was definitely coming from up above. I picked up a rotten apple and hurled it at the oak tree. There was a rustling in the leaves and then silence.

Suddenly Carlos jumped up from his seat. "Tariq, look out!"

I heard a loud SWOOSH and ducked just in time as a huge bird swooped down from the tree. Carlos rushed over to me. "Are you okay?"

I nodded and looked at the table where Carlos and I had been eating. The most unusual bird I had ever seen was perched on top. It sniffed at our cookies, then looked up at the sun and began to sing once more.

Carlos and I stared at the amazing bird. Its breast was covered with shiny gold feathers, and its wings were blue and green. The bird had a plume of brilliant red feathers on its head, and its beak looked like it was made of pure gold. All of a sudden the bird stopped singing and looked at us with its sparkling emerald eyes.

"What is it?" asked Carlos.

All I could do was shrug. The bird reminded me of an eagle, but it had satiny feathers like a peacock I saw once at the zoo. I wanted to say that maybe it was a magical bird, but I wasn't sure what Carlos would think.

Before I could say anything, the beautiful bird flew over our heads and perched on a branch of the pear tree. It cocked its head to one side and watched us again.

"C'mon," I said to Carlos as I pulled him away from the tree. "Let's get back to work."

The mysterious bird watched us while we cleaned up the yard. At first it made us kind of nervous, but after a while we forgot the strange bird was even there.

2.

By noon Carlos and I were tired, but there was still a lot of work to be done. We decided to go home and return later that afternoon. We slipped out of the yard when no one was looking and went to my house for lunch.

On our way back to the yard we saw one of our classmates walking up Barkley Street. Carlos waved to Vikram and called him over.

I pulled Carlos aside. "What are you doing?"

I hissed in his ear. "Do you want Vikram to find out about our secret hang-out spot?"

Carlos just gave me a laid back smile. "Relax, Tariq," he said.

Vikram crossed the street and joined us.

"Hey, Vik, where are you heading?" asked Carlos.

Vikram was carrying two heavy bags. "Home. I had to get some things from the store for my mom. Where are you guys going?"

I tried to act as cool as Carlos. "Nowhere," I said. "We're just hanging out."

For a moment the three of us just looked at one another. Finally Carlos spoke up. "Hey, Vik. You're a dinosaur expert, right?"

Vikram just shrugged and looked kind of embarrassed. I remembered Vik being really into dinosaurs when we were kids, but that was back in the day. Carlos went on. "Do you know anything about birds?"

"That depends," Vikram replied. "What kind of bird are you talking about?"

Carlos and I looked at each other. I knew what he was thinking. "C'mon," I said to Vikram. "There's something you got to see."

Once we were back inside the garden, Carlos and I looked around for the mysterious golden bird. Vikram set his grocery bags on the ground.

"Do either of you guys know how to make bird calls?" he asked.

Carlos and I began walking around the yard, whistling like birds. Vikram took a bag of potato chips out of his bag and went over to the patio. He put a handful of chips on the tabletop and then went back to the fence. Suddenly we heard a rustling up high in the oak tree. Carlos and I quickly got out of the way. All three of us held our breath and waited to see what would happen.

For a moment there was nothing but silence and then—SWOOSH! The huge bird swooped down and perched on the edge of the table. Vikram's eyes opened wide.

We watched to see if the strange bird would eat the potato chips. After pushing them around with its sharp gold beak, the bird seemed to shake its head. Then it just stared at us with its glittering green eyes.

Carlos nudged Vikram. "So, what do you think? What kind of bird is it?"

Vikram just stared at the strange bird as if he were drawing a picture of it in his mind. Suddenly Vikram picked up his bags and turned to go.

Carlos frowned at him. "You're leaving?"

Vikram glanced at the huge golden bird sitting

on the table. "I'm going home and then I'm heading to the library," he replied. "Will you guys still be here when I get back?"

I gave Vikram a dirty look. "You're not going to tell anyone, are you?"

Vikram shook his head. "Are you kidding? That's no ordinary bird, you guys. If I'm right, that bird should have been extinct thousands of years ago! I'm going to go do some research. Then I'll come back here and tell you what I've found. Deal?"

Carlos and I looked at each other. We had no choice but to trust Vikram. "Deal," we said.

Carlos and I made up a special signal for Vikram to use when he wanted back in—three knocks followed by three short whistle blows.

There was still a lot to be done, so Carlos and I put on our gardening gloves and went back to work. The golden bird watched us for a moment and then flew away.

A little while later we heard the special signal coming from the other side of the fence.

Carlos stopped raking and looked at me. "Is Vik back already?"

I went over to the fence. Something didn't seem right. I tried peeking through the narrow crack, but the ivy on the other side made it hard to see who was there. We heard the special signal once more.

"We'd better open up," whispered Carlos. "Maybe Vik forgot something."

Carlos and I pried the first plank off the fence. Before we realized what was happening, my little sister and her best friend pushed their way through the ivy and tumbled into the yard.

"I knew it!" Zaria shouted triumphantly. "I

knew you were up to something!"

I was so mad I felt like I was going to explode! Zaria was always an annoying pest and she had pulled some sneaky tricks before, but this was just *too much*.

Carlos could tell how angry I was. He put his hand on my arm. "Be cool, man. We'll get rid of them."

I tried to stay calm, but Zaria was already making plans for *our* secret hang-out spot! She and Lisette talked about bringing their skipping ropes into the yard along with more of their annoying friends.

I couldn't keep my anger inside any longer. "GET OUT!" I yelled as loud as I could. "And take your stupid friend with you!"

Zaria folded her arms across her chest and put on her low-down-mean-and-nasty look. "You can't tell me what to do in here, Tariq! This isn't your backyard. Lisette and I can stay here as long as we want. And if you try to make us leave, we'll tell everybody what you're up to—including Mom and Dad!"

I was about to lunge at Zaria when Carlos stepped between us. "Cool it, you two. If you keep yelling at each other, someone outside will hear and we'll ALL get thrown out of here."

I didn't want to share our secret hang-out spot with my bratty sister and her friend, but I knew Zaria would blab if we didn't let her stay. I looked at Carlos. He just shrugged and handed his gardening gloves to our unwanted guests.

"Here," Carlos said as he gave each of them a glove. "Make yourselves useful and pull up some of those weeds."

I picked up the shears and went to a far corner

of the yard. Carlos took up the rake again, and all
of us went back to work.

3.

An hour later, we heard the special signal coming from the other side of the fence. This time we knew it had to be Vikram. Carlos and I went to the fence and let him back into the yard.

"So what did you find out?" Carlos asked eagerly.

"Not much," said Vikram. "I couldn't find our mysterious bird in any of the books at the library."

Vikram looked around the yard for the golden bird, but instead he found Zaria and Lisette.

"What are they doing here?"

Carlos explained how the two girls had tricked us by using the special signal. I still didn't want them hanging around, but I had to admit that Zaria and Lisette were working hard. They had pulled up almost all of the weeds that were growing around the patio.

Zaria and Lisette sat down to take a break.

"Anybody want gum?" Lisette took a pack of blue gumballs out of her pocket. Zaria held out her hand.

Suddenly Carlos, Vikram, and I heard a rustling up in the oak tree. Before we could warn the girls, the golden bird swooped down from the tree.

SWOOSH!

When Lisette looked up and saw the huge golden bird soaring towards her, she dropped the pack of gum and put both hands over her mouth.

Zaria didn't know what was about to happen. She caught the falling gumballs and gave her friend a confused look. "What's wrong, Lisette?"

Carlos, Vikram, and I watched in amazement as the strange bird opened its gleaming silver talons and perched not on the edge of the table, but on Zaria's outstretched arm!

Zaria froze. "T-T-Tariq—"

I had never seen my little sister so scared before. The golden bird looked right at Zaria. Then it turned its head and looked at the blue gumballs Lisette had dropped into my sister's hand.

Vikram watched the mysterious bird as it moved its head back and forth. Suddenly he had an idea. "Zaria, drop the gum!"

Zaria did as she was told and four blue gumballs dropped onto the tabletop. Instantly the golden bird let go of Zaria's arm. It hovered in the air

and quickly gobbled up all four pieces of gum before even one could roll off the edge of the table.

Zaria and Lisette jumped up from their seats and ran over to where we were standing. We watched in amazement as the strange bird chewed and swallowed the four pieces of gum.

Vikram turned to Lisette. "Do you have any more?"

Lisette gave Vikram another pack of gum. Vikram opened it and threw a single red gumball high into the air. The rest of us watched in wonder as the golden bird soared into the sky and snatched the gumball out of the air with its beak. Vikram threw another gumball into the air and again the amazing bird caught the gum and swallowed it before landing on the table.

Next Vikram dumped the rest of the

gumballs into the palm of his hand. We watched breathlessly as Vikram knelt down with his hand held out before him. The strange bird looked at the gum in Vikram's hand, and then hopped off the table and onto the ground. It looked up at us with its emerald eyes. Then the golden bird took a step forward and cautiously snatched one of the gumballs out of Vikram's hand.

Carlos turned to me. "What kind of bird eats gum?"

I shrugged as the bird took another gumball from Vikram's hand. Zaria moved in closer and tried to touch the beautiful bird. Instead of flying away, the bird just looked up at her and calmly continued eating.

"Ooooh," said Zaria. "Her feathers feel just like silk. Touch her, Lisette."

Lisette reached out and touched one of the

bird's beautiful blue and green wings. Carlos lightly stroked the spray of red feathers on top of the bird's head.

I wanted to pet the bird, too, but I shoved my hands into my pockets instead. I liked it better when the yard and the mysterious bird had belonged only to Carlos and me. Part of me wished that Vikram, Zaria, and Lisette had never found out about our secret hang-out spot.

"She's so beautiful!" said Zaria admiringly.

I frowned and gave my sister a shove. "Shut up, Zaria. It's not a girl!"

Zaria stood up and shoved me back. "How do you know, Tariq? It could be a girl. You're just jealous because SHE likes ME better than YOU!"

I shoved Zaria again, harder this time. She bumped into Lisette and knocked her to the ground.

"Hey, watch out!" cried Lisette as she fell into the tall grass.

Zaria put on her low-down-mean-and-nasty look and punched me as hard as she could.

"Ooooof!" I doubled over and clutched my stomach.

Carlos grabbed Zaria's arm before she could punch me again. "Cool it, shorty."

Lisette jumped up and grabbed a handful of his hair. "Let go of my friend!"

"Stop it, you guys!" cried Vikram. He tried to break up the fight but we were too angry to stop.

Suddenly we heard a loud, shrill screech. "KRAI! KRAI! KRAI!"

The strange golden bird was hopping up and down and flapping its wings. Its emerald eyes were glowing. Over and over it made that awful sound until we all stopped fighting and covered our ears.

Finally, the bird settled down and was quiet once more. We looked at each other and felt ashamed.

"Maybe we should go home now," Carlos sheepishly suggested.

We all agreed to return the next day. We also promised not to tell anyone else about our secret hang-out spot. The strange golden bird flew up into the oak tree, and one by one we slipped out of the yard.

Carlos, Vikram, Lisette, Zaria, and I spent all day Sunday working in the yard. During the week we met after school and kept on working. Day after day we worked in the yard until it began to look like the perfect hang-out spot.

Each day while we worked, the strange golden bird watched us with its sparkling green eyes. Sometimes it would stop singing to listen to our conversation. We took turns bringing gumballs to feed our new feathery friend.

On Friday our class took a trip to the museum. When it was time for lunch, Vikram pulled us aside. "Hey, you guys. Want to go see the mummies?"

We left the rest of the class and followed Vikram to the Egyptian exhibit. We looked at the spooky mummies and the glittering gold face masks of the pharaohs.

"Hey, check this out!"

Carlos called us over to a glass cabinet that held a tattered piece of papyrus. The ancient yellow paper was covered with hieroglyphs and strange pictures of people and animals. In the very middle there was a painting of a beautiful golden bird. Its blue and green wings were open wide, and there was a plume of red feathers on its head.

"That's it!" I exclaimed. "That's our bird!"

Suddenly a security guard came up to us. "Are

you boys lost?" he asked.

We looked at each other. Carlos spoke up first. "Um—we got separated from our class."

The security guard smiled at us. "I see," he said. Then he pointed at the painting of the golden bird. "Do you boys know what kind of bird that is?"

We shook our heads.

"That's a phoenix," said the security guard. "According to the ancient Egyptians, every five hundred years the phoenix made itself a nest, filled it with special spices, and then set the whole thing on fire."

"Why would a bird set its own nest on fire?" I asked.

"Well," said the security guard, "that's what the phoenix did when it was ready to start a new life. The old bird died in the flames, but then a new

bird was born out of the ashes. For the Egyptians, the phoenix was an important symbol of life after death."

Carlos, Vikram, and I looked at one another. Could the mysterious bird in our yard be a phoenix? We thanked the friendly security guard for the information and went to join our class.

After school, instead of going straight to our secret hang-out spot, the three of us went to the library. We signed up for a computer and tried to find out more about the phoenix on the Internet. The more we learned, the more convinced we became that the golden bird living in the oak tree really was a phoenix! We headed to our secret hang-out spot to tell Zaria and Lisette what we'd learned.

On our way to the yard, we ran into Carlos's cousin Felipe. Felipe was older than us. Sometimes he hung out with the teenage boys in the park. Felipe wore a white bandana tied around his head. Carlos once told me he thought his cousin was part of a gang.

Felipe smiled and came up to us. "Hey, you guys. What's up?"

"Nothing much," we said. We didn't want Felipe to find out about our secret hang-out spot.

Felipe put his arm around Carlos. "Hey, Cuz, why don't you and your friends come hang out with us in the park?"

Carlos looked down at the ground and shook his head.

"Why not?" asked Felipe. "You got something better to do?"

Carlos wasn't sure what to say. He bit his lip and looked at me.

"Uh—we have a project to work on for school," I said.

Vikram nodded. "Yeah, it's on ancient Egypt."

Felipe laughed at us. "School is for losers," he said. "You guys should forget about doing your homework and come meet my friend Rashid. He never goes to school and he's the smartest guy I know."

Carlos shrugged off Felipe's arm. "We got to go," he said. Vikram and I followed Carlos down Barkley Street.

When we reached our secret hang-out spot, we made the special signal and Zaria and Lisette let us into the yard. The phoenix heard our voices and flew down from the oak tree. Carlos, Vikram, and I told the girls everything we had learned about the mysterious golden bird.

Zaria began stroking its silky feathers. "Are you sure this is a phoenix? She doesn't look like she's five hundred years old."

Vikram took some gum out of his pocket and began to feed the golden bird. "She may not be five hundred years old, but she's a phoenix, alright. She looks just like the picture we saw at the museum."

I nodded. "Plus the website we found said that the phoenix makes its nest in an oak tree and eats 'odoriferous' gum."

"What does that mean?" asked Lisette.

"Gum that smells good," answered Carlos.

We grew quiet as we took turns feeding the golden phoenix. All of us wondered if the beautiful bird would someday set its nest on fire and perish in the flames.

"Maybe she's a baby bird," said Zaria hopefully.

Lisette nodded excitedly. "Maybe she's only a hundred years old! That means she'll be around for a long, long time."

All of a sudden we heard loud voices coming from the other side of the fence. We heard laughter, then the rattle of spray cans being shaken and the hiss of paint being sprayed on the fence.

We held our breath and looked at one another. Who would vandalize our secret hang-out spot? Would they find a way to break into the yard? Did they know we were inside?

I listened to the vandals to see if I could recognize their voices. They sounded like some of the older boys who usually hung out in the park. One of the boys sounded like Felipe.

Suddenly an empty bottle was tossed over the fence. It landed near us and smashed into pieces. We began to feel afraid. We weren't sure what would happen next.

I looked at the golden phoenix. Its emerald eyes began to glow. "KRAI! KRAI!"

We covered our ears as the phoenix flapped its wings and lifted itself into the air. It hovered just above the fence and continued to screech at the vandals. "KRAI! KRAI! KRAI!"

For a moment the spraying and the laughter stopped. Then a mean voice cried out, "Shut up, you stupid bird!"

One of the vandals hurled an empty spray can at the phoenix. It missed the bird and sailed over the fence. We huddled under the table for protection.

The phoenix continued to screech angrily. Another spray can flew over the fence followed by a shower of rocks and bottles. Suddenly a large stone struck the phoenix. It cried out before falling to the ground.

The vandals laughed and cheered. They kicked the fence, threw some more trash into the yard, and then went away.

We rushed over to our fallen friend. The phoenix lay motionless on the ground, its emerald eyes shut tight.

Lisette began to cry softly. Zaria put an arm around her friend and looked at me with tears in her eyes. "Is she dead?"

I swallowed hard and looked at Carlos. I wasn't sure what to do. I knelt down beside the phoenix and gently stroked its golden head.

Vikram knelt beside me and put his ear close to the bird's breast. "I can still hear a heartbeat," he said.

Slowly the phoenix opened its eyes. It shook its head and struggled to its feet. We stood back and anxiously watched our feathery friend. The golden bird stretched out its wings and took a few wobbly steps toward the oak tree. Then the phoenix turned and looked at us. Its eyes were dark and sad.

"Are you alright?" asked Zaria.

The phoenix made no reply. It simply spread its beautiful blue and green wings and flew away.

Without speaking we gathered up all the trash the vandals had thrown over the fence. When we were sure no one was looking, we slipped out of the yard.

We could hardly believe our eyes. The curtain of ivy had been torn from the fence, and the old wooden planks were covered with red and black paint. Carlos scowled fiercely as he looked at the ugly words and symbols. I knew he was thinking of his cousin Felipe.

It was getting late. We agreed to meet again early the next morning. Then we said goodbye to each other and went home.

When we reached our secret hang-out spot the next day, even more graffiti had been sprayed on the fence.

"Do you think they figured out how to get in?" Carlos asked nervously.

I sighed grimly. "There's only one way to find out."

We looked around to make sure no one was watching. Then we pried off the loose planks and crept into the yard.

Our hearts sank when we saw what they had done to our secret hang-out spot. We had spent weeks fixing up the abandoned yard, and overnight the vandals had ruined everything.

"Where's the phoenix?" asked Zaria.

We began looking for our golden friend. Carlos and Vikram made birdcalls. Zaria and Lisette sifted through the trash that littered the ground.

I walked over to the old oak tree. Broken branches were scattered all around. Something shiny caught my eye. I moved some of the branches aside and saw what looked like part of a nest. Matted clumps of twigs and straw lay on the ground along with three silver bundles.

Vikram came up beside me. "What did you find?" he asked.

I picked up one of the bundles. I peeled away the silver foil and smelled the slender sticks. "It's incense," I replied.

I yelled over my shoulder, "Hey, Carlos! Come check this out!" But when I turned around, Carlos was gone.

"Where did he go?" I asked.

"He looked kind of angry," said Zaria. "Maybe he went home."

I remembered how upset Carlos had been last night. We knew that his cousin Felipe was one of the vandals who had destroyed our secret hang-out spot.

I rushed over to the fence and let myself out into the street. I raced toward the park, but halfway up Barkley Street I ran into a group of teenage boys. Carlos was with them and so was Felipe. All of the older boys had white bandanas tied around their heads.

I stood next to my best friend. I had never seen

Carlos so angry before. He yelled at his cousin. "WHY? Why did you do it?"

Felipe didn't say anything. He just turned away and looked at the ground. Another boy stepped forward. A gold chain hung around his neck. I knew this was Rashid, the leader of the gang.

"I hear you boys want to join our crew." Rashid smiled and his teeth glittered with gold.

"No way," I said. "We want to know why you wrecked our hang-out spot."

Rashid threw his head back and laughed. "C'mon, boys, I want to show you something."

We went to the end of the block and turned the corner. Rashid stopped in front of the old wooden fence. He pointed to a red and black symbol the vandals had made with spray paint.

"See that? That's the mark of the Pythons. This building belongs to us now, and this yard is Python territory."

"This is OUR yard!" Carlos said defiantly. "We're the ones who found it, and we're the ones who fixed it up."

Rashid and the other gang members just laughed. Rashid pounded on the fence with his fist. Someone inside the yard removed the secret planks. Carlos and I followed Rashid into the yard.

Other gang members were already inside. Vikram, Zaria, and Lisette were standing together under the oak tree. They looked scared.

Rashid smirked as he surveyed the damage his gang had caused. "What a dump! This is what you call a hang-out spot?"

My cheeks started to burn. "It wasn't a dump until your gang broke in and trashed it! You guys have ruined everything—first the park, and now our yard."

Rashid put his arm around me and Carlos.

"You'd see things differently if you were one of us. Why don't you join our crew? If you become a Python, nobody will ever mess with you. And we'll let you hang out here with us."

Zaria pulled me away from Rashid. She put on her low-down-mean-and-nasty look. "Leave my brother alone. Nobody wants to join your stupid gang!"

Rashid gave Zaria a dirty look. "I wasn't talking to you, shorty. Girls aren't allowed in the Pythons, anyway. So why don't you just STEP!"

Rashid pushed my little sister. Zaria stumbled and fell against the fence.

My anger boiled over. I shoved Rashid as hard as I could.

"GET OUT!" I yelled. "You've ruined everything! Just GET OUT!"

Rashid fell backwards. He tripped over a

broken branch and fell to the ground.

"Ow!" Rashid looked at his hand. He had cut it on some broken glass.

The other gang members grabbed me and Vikram. Carlos tried to help us, but two older boys held his arms. Lisette and Zaria slipped through the fence and ran for help.

Rashid glared at us. "I've had enough of you little punks. Nobody messes with the Pythons." Rashid picked up the broken bottle.

Carlos turned to his cousin. "Felipe, help us!"

Felipe wasn't sure what to do. He looked at us, then at the other members of his gang. Finally he grabbed Rashid's arm. "Let them go, man. They're just kids."

Rashid tried to pull his arm away. "Don't tell me what to do. I'M the leader of this gang!" The two boys began wrestling with each other.

Carlos broke free and tried to help his cousin. Rashid spun around. The broken bottle slashed across Carlos's arm.

I yelled as loud as I could, "HELP! Somebody help us!"

Suddenly a shrill screech pierced the air. "KRAAAIIIII!"

We all looked up into the sky. For a moment it seemed as if the sun had disappeared. Dark clouds loomed overhead and strange, spicy smoke filled the air. We heard another screech and then— SWOOSH—the golden phoenix appeared!

It hovered above us with its emerald eyes glowing, and its blue and green wings open wide. Several silver bundles were grasped between its sharp talons, and its gold beak flashed like lightning as the phoenix continued to screech. "KRAI! KRAI! KRAI!"

Against the dark grey clouds, the phoenix shone as bright as the sun. I put my hand up to shield my eyes and that's when I realized that the phoenix was on fire! Flames were shooting off the tips of its wings and its tail was burning like a torch. Each time the phoenix flapped its wings, the flames grew bigger and fiery feathers fell to the ground.

Several of the gang members got scared and ran out of the yard. Rashid was trembling with anger and fear, but he still refused to leave. Instead he hurled the broken bottle at the flaming bird. "I'm not afraid of you!" he yelled.

The phoenix quickly dropped the silver bundles and caught the bottle in its claw. It screeched once more, then crushed the bottle between its sharp talons. Glass fell down on us like rain.

Rashid bent to pick up a stone but before

he could throw it, the phoenix swooped down on him. It grabbed Rashid by the shoulders and shook him soundly before throwing him to the ground.

The yard was filled with smoke. The fruit trees were on fire, and the abandoned building was burning as well. We could hear the loud siren of a fire engine coming down Barkley Street.

Vikram and I covered our mouths and rushed over to Carlos. He lay on the ground clutching his arm. We helped him get up and carried him over to the fence. Felipe pulled off more of the old wooden planks and we escaped into the street.

When it was Felipe's turn to squeeze through the fence, he paused. He turned around and looked for the leader of his gang. Rashid was trying to crawl to safety but he couldn't see through the thick black smoke.

Felipe took off his white bandana and tied it around his face. He rushed back into the yard and grabbed Rashid. The two boys stumbled toward the fence and fell onto the sidewalk, coughing and gasping for air.

Zaria and Lisette rushed over to us, followed by our parents and some of our neighbors. We stood together on the opposite side of the street and watched as flames devoured the old abandoned building. Thick plumes of smoke rose above the wooden fence. For an instant we saw the flash of two emerald eyes. Then we heard the phoenix utter one last cry and the glowing eyes disappeared.

6.

After the fire, things weren't the same on Barkley Street. At first, we all felt sad. We had lost our secret hang-out spot *and* our special friend. But we knew that from the ashes a young phoenix had been born. And we all hoped the new bird would find a safe place to live for another five hundred years.

For several weeks the empty lot remained hidden behind a tall aluminum fence. Then some

of the families on Barkley Street got together and formed a block association. We were all tired of the gangs, the graffiti, and the garbage that was ruining our neighborhood. So we decided to do something about it...

Carlos and I hang out in the community garden almost every day. It's even better than our old hang-out spot, and everyone on our block gets to enjoy it.

We still miss the phoenix. But sometimes, when the wind blows down Barkley Street, we smell that spicy incense and all of us remember our beautiful golden friend.

59

Discussion Guide

1. Describe your ideal hang-out spot. Are there safe spaces for you to hang out in your neighborhood? If not, how and where could you create a new hang-out spot?

2. The children learn that the ancient phoenix likes some things and dislikes others. Make a list of things the phoenix needs to be happy.

3. There are firebirds in many different cultures. The ancient Egyptians called theirs the Bennu bird. Find a picture of the Egyptian phoenix. How is it different from the phoenix in this book?

4. Felipe is torn between his loyalty to his cousin Carlos and his loyalty to the Pythons. Why do you think he joined the gang? What do you think will happen to Felipe after the fire?

5. The abandoned brownstone becomes a community garden after the fire. If a new bird always rises from the ashes, what do you think happened to the newborn phoenix?

about the author

Born in Canada, Zetta Elliott moved to the US in 1994. Her books for young readers include the award-winning picture book *Bird*, *Ship of Souls*, *The Boy in the Bubble* and *Max Loves Muñecas!* She lives in Brooklyn and likes birds, glitter, and other magical things.

Learn more at www.zettaelliott.com

Silver Falls Library
410 S. Water St.
Silverton, OR 97381
(503) 873-5173

9 781500 589400